INTRODUCING...

Girl

Philip
Gregg

William
Gregg

Mr and Mrs
Gregg

ROALD DAHL

The Magic Finger

Illustrated by Quentin Blake

PUFFIN

Find out more about Roald Dahl
by visiting the web site at
www.roalddahl.com

PUFFIN BOOKS

Published by the Penguin Group
Penguin Books Ltd, 80 Strand, London WC2R 0RL, England
Penguin Group (USA), Inc., 375 Hudson Street, New York, New York 10014, USA
Penguin Books Australia Ltd, 250 Camberwell Road, Camberwell, Victoria 3124, Australia
Penguin Books Canada Ltd, 10 Alcorn Avenue, Toronto, Ontario, Canada M4V 3B2
Penguin Books India (P) Ltd, 11 Community Centre, Panchsheel Park,
New Delhi – 110 017, India
Penguin Group (NZ), cnr Airborne and Rosedale Roads, Albany, Auckland 1310,
New Zealand
Penguin Books (South Africa) (Pty) Ltd, 24 Sturdee Avenue, Rosebank 2196, South Africa

Penguin Books Ltd, Registered Offices: 80 Strand, London WC2R 0RL, England

www.penguin.com

First published in the USA 1966
First published in Great Britain by George Allen and Unwin 1968
Published in Puffin Books 1974
Reissued with new illustrations 1995
This edition has been produced exclusively for Nestlé breakfast cereals 2004
1

Text copyright © Roald Dahl Nominee Ltd, 1966
Illustrations copyright © Quentin Blake, 1995
All rights reserved

The moral right of the illustrator has been asserted

Set in Monotype Baskerville

Made and printed in England by Clays Ltd, St Ives plc

British Library Cataloguing in Publication Data
A CIP catalogue record for this book is available from the British Library

ISBN 0–141–31898–8

This book is for Ophelia and Lucy

The farm next to ours is owned by Mr and Mrs Gregg. The Greggs have two children, both of them boys. Their names are Philip and William. Sometimes I go over to their farm to play with them.

I am a girl and I am eight years old.

Philip is also eight years old.

William is three years older. He is ten.

What?

Oh, all right, then.

He is eleven.

Last week, something very funny happened to the Gregg family. I am going to tell you about it as best I can.

Now the one thing that Mr Gregg and his two boys loved to do more than anything else was to go hunting. Every Saturday morning they would take their guns and go off into the woods to look for animals and birds to shoot. Even Philip, who was only eight years old, had a gun of his own.

I can't stand hunting. I just can't *stand* it. It doesn't seem right to me that men and boys should kill animals just for the fun they get out of it. So I used to try to stop Philip and William from doing it. Every time I went over to their farm I would do my best to talk them out of it, but they only laughed at me.

I even said something about it once to Mr Gregg, but he just walked on past me as if I weren't there.

Then, one Saturday morning, I saw Philip and William coming out of the woods with their father, and they were carrying a lovely young deer.

This made me so cross that I started shouting at them.

The boys laughed and made faces at me, and Mr Gregg told me to go home and mind my own P's and Q's.

Well, that did it!

I saw red.

And before I was able to stop myself, I did something I never meant to do.

I PUT THE MAGIC FINGER ON THEM ALL!

Oh, dear! Oh, dear! I even put it on Mrs Gregg, who wasn't there. I put it on the whole Gregg family.

For months I had been telling myself that I would never put the Magic Finger upon anyone again – not after what happened to my teacher, old Mrs Winter.

Poor old Mrs Winter.

One day we were in class, and she was teaching us spelling. 'Stand up,' she said to me, 'and spell cat.'

'That's an easy one,' I said. *'K-a-t.'*

'You are a stupid little girl!' Mrs Winter said.

'I am not a stupid little girl!' I cried. 'I am a very nice little girl!'

'Go and stand in the corner,' Mrs Winter said.

Then I got cross, and I saw red, and I put the Magic Finger on Mrs Winter good and strong, and almost at once . . .

Guess what?

Whiskers began growing out of her face! They were long black whiskers, just like the ones you see on a cat, only much bigger. And how fast they grew! Before we had time to think, they were out to her ears!

Of course the whole class started screaming with laughter, and then Mrs Winter said, 'Will you be so kind as to tell me what you find so madly funny, all of you?'

And when she turned around to write something on the blackboard we saw that she had grown a *tail* as well! It was a huge bushy tail!

I cannot begin to tell you what happened after that, but if any of you are wondering whether Mrs Winter is quite all right again now, the answer is No. And she never will be.

The Magic Finger is something I have been able to do all my life.

I can't tell you just *how* I do it, because I don't even know myself.

But it always happens when I get cross, when I see red . . .

Then I get very, very hot all over . . .

Then the tip of the forefinger of my right hand begins to tingle most terribly . . .

And suddenly a sort of flash comes out of me, a quick flash, like something electric.

It jumps out and touches the person who has made me cross . . .

And after that the Magic Finger is upon him or her, and things begin to happen . . .

Well, the Magic Finger was now upon the whole of the Gregg family, and there was no taking it off again.

I ran home and waited for things to happen.

They happened fast.

I shall now tell you what those things were. I got the whole story from Philip and William the next morning, after it was all over.

In the afternoon of the very same day that I put the Magic Finger on the Gregg family, Mr Gregg and Philip and William went out hunting once again. This time they were going after wild ducks, so they headed towards the lake.

In the first hour they got ten birds.

In the next hour they got another six.

'What a day!' cried Mr Gregg. 'This is the best yet!' He was beside himself with joy.

Just then four more wild ducks flew over their heads. They were flying very low. They were easy to hit.

BANG! BANG! BANG! BANG! went the guns.

The ducks flew on.

'We missed!' said Mr Gregg. 'That's funny.'

Then, to everyone's surprise, the four ducks turned around and came flying right back to the guns.

'Hey!' said Mr Gregg. 'What on earth are they doing? They are really asking for it this time!' He shot at them again. So did the boys. And again they all missed!

Mr Gregg got very red in the face. 'It's the light,' he said. 'It's getting too dark to see. Let's go home.'

So they started for home, carrying with them the sixteen birds they had shot before.

But the four ducks would not leave them alone. They now began flying around and around the hunters as they walked away.

Mr Gregg did not like it one bit. 'Be off!' he cried, and he shot at them many more times, but it was no good. He simply could not hit them. All the way home those four ducks flew around in the sky above their heads, and nothing would make them go away.

Late that night, after Philip and William had gone to bed, Mr Gregg went outside to get some wood for the fire.

He was crossing the yard when all at once he heard the call of a wild duck in the sky.

He stopped and looked up. The night was very still. There was a thin yellow moon over the trees on the hill, and the sky was filled with stars. Then Mr Gregg heard the noise of wings flying low over his head, and he saw the four ducks, dark against the night sky, flying very close together. They were going around and around the house.

Mr Gregg forgot about the firewood, and hurried back indoors. He was now quite afraid. He did not like what was going on. But he said nothing about it to Mrs Gregg. All he said was, 'Come on, let's go to bed. I feel tired.'

So they went to bed and to sleep.

When morning came, Mr Gregg was the first to wake up.

He opened his eyes.

He was about to put out a hand for his watch, to see the time.

But his hand wouldn't come out.

'That's funny,' he said. 'Where is my hand?'

He lay still, wondering what was up.

Maybe he had hurt that hand in some way?

He tried the other hand.

That wouldn't come out either.

He sat up.

Then, for the first time, he saw what he looked like!

He gave a yell and jumped out of bed.

Mrs Gregg woke up. And when she saw Mr Gregg standing there on the floor, *she* gave a yell, too.

For he was now a tiny little man!

He was maybe as tall as the seat of a chair, but no taller.

And where his arms had been, he had a pair of duck's wings instead!

'But . . . but . . . but . . .' cried Mrs Gregg, going purple in the face. 'My dear man, what's happened to you?'

'What's happened to both of us, you mean!' shouted Mr Gregg.

It was Mrs Gregg's turn now to jump out of bed.

She ran to look at herself in the glass. But she was not tall enough to see into it. She was even smaller than Mr Gregg, and she, too, had got wings instead of arms.

'Oh! Oh! Oh! Oh!' sobbed Mrs Gregg.

'This is witches' work!' cried Mr Gregg. And both of them started running around the room, flapping their wings.

A minute later Philip and William burst in. The same thing had happened to them. They had wings and no arms. And they were *really* tiny. They were about as big as robins.

'Mama! Mama! Mama!' chirruped Philip. 'Look, Mama, we can fly!' And they flew up into the air.

'Come down at once!' said Mrs Gregg. 'You're much too high!' But before she could say another word, Philip and William had flown right out the window.

Mr and Mrs Gregg ran to the window and looked out. The two tiny boys were now high up in the sky.

Then Mrs Gregg said to Mr Gregg, 'Do you think *we* could do that, my dear?'

'I don't see why not,' Mr Gregg said. 'Come on, let's try.'

Mr Gregg began to flap his wings hard, and all at once, up he went.

Then Mrs Gregg did the same.

'Help!' she cried as she started going up. 'Save me!'

'Come on,' said Mr Gregg. 'Don't be afraid.'

So out the window they flew, far up into the sky, and it did not take them long to catch up with Philip and William.

Soon the whole family was flying around and around together.

'Oh, isn't it lovely!' cried William. 'I've always wanted to know what it feels like to be a bird!'

'Your wings are not getting tired, are they, dear?' Mr Gregg asked Mrs Gregg.

'Not at all,' Mrs Gregg said. 'I could go on for ever!'

'Hey, look down there!' said Philip. 'Somebody is walking in our garden!'

They all looked down, and there below them, in their own garden, they saw four *enormous* wild ducks! The ducks were as big as men, and what is more, they had great long arms, like men, instead of wings.

The ducks were walking in a line to the door of the Greggs' house, swinging their arms and holding their beaks high in the air.

'Stop!' called the tiny Mr Gregg, flying down low over their heads. 'Go away! That's my house!'

The ducks looked up and quacked. The first one put out a hand and opened the door of the house and went in. The others went in after him. The door shut.

The Greggs flew down and sat on the wall near the door. Mrs Gregg began to cry.

'Oh, dear! Oh, dear!' she sobbed. 'They have taken our house. What *shall* we do? We have no place to go!'

Even the boys began to cry a bit now.

'We will be eaten by cats and foxes in the night!' said Philip.

'I want to sleep in my own bed!' said William.

'Now then,' said Mr Gregg. 'It isn't any good crying. That won't help us. Shall I tell you what we are going to do?'

'What?' they said.

Mr Gregg looked at them and smiled. 'We are going to build a nest.'

'A nest!' they said. 'Can we do that?'

'We *must* do it,' said Mr Gregg. 'We've got to have somewhere to sleep. Follow me.'

They flew off to a tall tree, and right at the top of it Mr Gregg chose the place for the nest.

'Now we want sticks,' he said. 'Lots and lots of little sticks. Off you go, all of you, and find them and bring them back here.'

'But we have no hands!' said Philip.

'Then use your mouths.'

Mrs Gregg and the children flew off. Soon they were back, carrying sticks in their mouths.

Mr Gregg took the sticks and started to build the nest.

'More,' he said. 'I want more and more and more sticks. Keep going.'

The nest began to grow. Mr Gregg was very good at making the sticks stick together.

After a while he said, 'That's enough sticks. Now I want leaves and feathers and things like that to make the inside nice and soft.'

The building of the nest went on and on. It took a long time. But at last it was finished.

'Try it,' said Mr Gregg, hopping back. He was very pleased with his work.

'Oh, isn't it lovely!' cried Mrs Gregg, going into it and sitting down. 'I feel I might lay an egg any moment!'

The others all got in beside her.

'How warm it is!' said William.

'And what fun to be living so high up,' said Philip. 'We may be small, but nobody can hurt us up here.'

'But what about food?' said Mrs Gregg. 'We haven't had a thing to eat all day.'

'That's right,' Mr Gregg said. 'So we will now fly back to the house and go in by an open window and get the tin of biscuits when the ducks aren't looking.'

'Oh, we will be pecked to bits by those dirty great ducks!' cried Mrs Gregg.

'We shall be very careful, my love,' said Mr Gregg. And off they went.

But when they got to the house, they found all the windows and doors closed. There was no way in.

'Just look at that beastly duck cooking at my stove!' cried Mrs Gregg as she flew past the kitchen window. 'How dare she!'

'And look at *that* one holding my lovely gun!' shouted Mr Gregg.

'One of them is lying in my bed!' yelled William, looking into a top window.

'And one of them is playing with my electric train!' cried Philip.

'Oh, dear! Oh, dear!' said Mrs Gregg. 'They have taken over our whole house! We shall never get it back. And what *are* we going to eat?'

'I will *not* eat worms,' said Philip. 'I would rather die.'

'Or slugs,' said William.

Mrs Gregg took the two boys under her wings and hugged them. 'Don't worry,' she said. 'I can mince it all up very fine and you won't even know the difference. Lovely slugburgers. Delicious wormburgers.'

'Oh no!' cried William.

'Never!' said Philip.

'Disgusting!' said Mr Gregg. 'Just because we have wings, we don't have to eat bird food. We shall eat apples instead. Our trees are full of them. Come on!'

So they flew off to an apple tree.

But to eat an apple without holding it in your hands is not at all easy. Every time you try to get your teeth into it, it just pushes away. In the end, they were able to get a few small bites each. And then it began to get dark, so they all flew back to the nest and lay down to sleep.

It must have been at about this time that I, back in my own house, picked up the telephone and tried to call Philip. I wanted to see if the family was all right.

'Hello,' I said.

'Quack!' said a voice at the other end.

'Who is it?' I asked.

'Quack-quack!'

'Philip,' I said, 'is that you?'

'Quack-quack-quack-quack-quack!'

'Oh, stop it!' I said.

Then there came a very funny noise. It was like a bird laughing.

I put down the telephone quickly.

'Oh, that Magic Finger!' I cried. 'What *has* it done to my friends?'

That night, while Mr and Mrs Gregg and Philip and William were trying to get some sleep up in the high nest, a great wind began to blow. The tree rocked from side to side, and everyone, even Mr

Gregg, was afraid that the nest would fall down.
Then came the rain. It rained and rained, and the
water ran into the nest and they all got as wet as
could be – and oh, it was a bad, bad night!

At last the morning came, and with it the warm sun.

'Well!' said Mrs Gregg. 'Thank goodness that's over! I never want to sleep in a nest again!' She got up and looked over the side . . .

'Help!' she cried. 'Look! Look down there!'

'What is it, my love?' said Mr Gregg. He stood up and peeped over the side.

He got the surprise of his life!

On the ground below them stood the four enormous ducks, as tall as men, and three of them were holding guns in their hands. One had Mr Gregg's gun, one had Philip's gun, and one had William's gun.

The guns were all pointing right up at the nest.

'No! No! No!' called out Mr and Mrs Gregg, both together. 'Don't shoot! Please don't shoot!'

'Why not?' said one of the ducks. It was the one who wasn't holding a gun. 'You are always shooting at *us*.'

'Oh, but that's not the same!' said Mr Gregg. 'We are *allowed* to shoot ducks!'

'Who allows you?' asked the duck.

'We allow each other,' said Mr Gregg.

'Very nice,' said the duck. 'And now *we* are going to allow each other to shoot you.'

(I would have loved to have seen Mr Gregg's face just then.)

'Oh, *please*!' cried Mrs Gregg. 'My two little children are up here with us! You wouldn't shoot my *children*!'

'Yesterday you shot *my* children,' said the duck. 'You shot all six of my children.'

'I'll never do it again!' cried Mr Gregg. 'Never, never, never!'

'Do you really mean that?' asked the duck.

'I *do* mean it!' said Mr Gregg. 'I'll never shoot another duck as long as I live!'

'That is not good enough,' said the duck. 'What about deer?'

'I'll do anything you say if you will only put down those guns!' cried Mr Gregg. 'I'll never shoot another duck or another deer or anything else again!'

'Will you give me your word on that?' said the duck.

'I will! I will!' said Mr Gregg.

'Will you throw away your guns?' asked the duck.

'I will break them into tiny bits!' said Mr Gregg. 'And never again need you be afraid of me or my family.'

'Very well,' said the duck. 'You may now come down. And by the way, may I congratulate you on the nest. For a first effort it's pretty good.'

Mr and Mrs Gregg and Philip and William hopped out of the nest and flew down.

Then all at once everything went black before their eyes, and they couldn't see. At the same time

a funny feeling came over them all, and they heard
a great wind blowing in their ears.

Then the black that was before their eyes turned to blue, to green, to red, and then to gold, and suddenly, there they were, standing in lovely bright sunshine in their own garden, near their own house, and everything was back to normal once again.

'Our wings have gone!' cried Mr Gregg. 'And our arms have come back!'

'And we are not tiny any more!' laughed Mrs Gregg. 'Oh, I am so glad!'

Philip and William began dancing about with joy.

Then, high above their heads, they heard the call of a wild duck. They all looked up, and they saw the four birds, lovely against the blue sky, flying very close together, heading back to the lake in the woods.

It must have been about half an hour later that I myself walked into the Greggs' garden. I had come to see how things were going, and I must admit I was expecting the worst. At the gate I stopped and stared. It was a queer sight.

In one corner Mr Gregg was smashing all three guns into tiny pieces with a huge hammer.

In another corner Mrs Gregg was placing beautiful flowers upon sixteen tiny mounds of soil which I learned later were the graves of the ducks that had been shot the day before.

And in the middle of the yard stood Philip and William, with a sack of their father's best barley beside them. They were surrounded by ducks, doves, pigeons, sparrows, robins, larks, and many other kinds that I did not know, and the birds were eating the barley that the boys were scattering by the handful.

'Good morning, Mr Gregg,' I said.

Mr Gregg lowered his hammer and looked at me. 'My name is not Gregg any more,' he said. 'In honour of my feathered friends, I have changed it from Gregg to Egg.'

'And I am Mrs Egg,' said Mrs Gregg.

'What happened?' I asked. They seemed to have gone completely dotty, all four of them.

Philip and William then began to tell me the whole story. When they had finished, William said, 'Look! There's the nest! Can you see it? Right up in the top of the tree! That's where we slept last night!'

'I built it *all* myself,' Mr Egg said proudly. 'Every stick of it.'

'If you don't believe us,' Mrs Egg said, 'just go into the house and take a look at the bathroom. It's a mess.'

'They filled the tub right up to the brim,' Philip said. 'They must have been swimming around in it all night! And feathers everywhere!'

'Ducks like water,' Mr Egg said. 'I'm glad they had a good time.'

Just then, from somewhere over by the lake, there came a loud BANG!

'Someone's shooting!' I cried.

'That'll be Jim Cooper,' Mr Egg said. 'Him and his three boys. They're shooting mad, those Coopers are, the whole family.'

Suddenly I started to see red . . .

Then I got very hot all over . . .

Then the tip of my finger began tingling most terribly. I could feel the power building up and up inside me . . .

I turned and started running towards the lake as fast as I could.

'Hey!' shouted Mr Egg. 'What's up? Where are you going?'

'To find the Coopers,' I called back.

'But why?'

'You wait and see!' I said. 'They'll be nesting in the trees tonight, every one of them!'

ROALD DAHL

BORN: Llandaff, Wales, 1916.
SCHOOLS: Llandaff Cathedral School,
St Peter's, Repton.
JOBS: Shell Oil Company representative in
East Africa, RAF fighter pilot in Second
World War, air attaché, author.

When Roald Dahl's own children were small, they used to keep a pet tortoise or two in the garden. This was long before they made it illegal to bring tortoises into England. As well as a writer, Dahl was a keen inventor and he did actually build the tortoise-catcher in this story – except that he used it for picking things up from the floor, to save bending his aching back!

Roald Dahl died in 1990 at the age of seventy-four.

This was the motto that he lived by:

My candle burns at both ends
It will not last the night
But ah my foes and oh my friends
It gives a lovely light.

Find out more about Roald Dahl by visiting the web site at
www.roalddahl.com

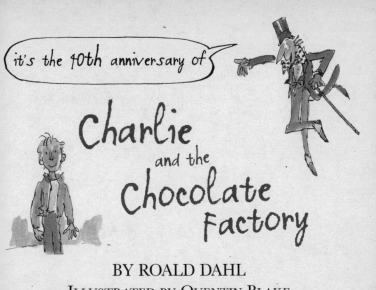

it's the 40th anniversary of

Charlie and the Chocolate Factory

BY ROALD DAHL
ILLUSTRATED BY QUENTIN BLAKE

Charlie and the Chocolate Factory was first published in 1964. It has achieved phenomenal success all over the world and continues to sell hundreds of thousands of copies every year - and that's just in the UK! Forty years on, it truly remains one of the most popular children's books of all time.

To celebrate, Puffin are publishing a gloriously scrumptious 40th anniversary edition to keep and treasure for at least another forty chocolate-filled years!

And if you've never read **Charlie and the Chocolate Factory** (gasp!) read on for a mouth-watering, chocolatey taste of what you've been missing . . .

I

Here Comes Charlie

These two very old people are the father and mother of Mr Bucket. Their names are Grandpa Joe and Grandma Josephine.

And *these* two very old people are the father and
mother of Mrs Bucket. Their names are Grandpa
George and Grandma Georgina.

This is Mr Bucket. This is Mrs Bucket.
Mr and Mrs Bucket have a small boy whose
name is Charlie Bucket.

This is Charlie.

How d'you do? And how d'you do? And how d'you do again? He is pleased to meet you.

The whole of this family – the six grown-ups (count them) and little Charlie Bucket – live together in a small wooden house on the edge of a great town.

The house wasn't nearly large enough for so many people, and life was extremely uncomfortable for them all. There were only two rooms in the place altogether, and there was only one bed. The bed was given to the four old grandparents because they were so old and tired. They were so tired, they never got out of it.

Grandpa Joe and Grandma Josephine on this side, Grandpa George and Grandma Georgina on this side.

Mr and Mrs Bucket and little Charlie Bucket slept in the other room, upon mattresses on the floor.

In the summertime, this wasn't too bad, but in the winter, freezing cold draughts blew across the floor all night long, and it was awful.

There wasn't any question of them being able to buy a better house – or even one more bed to sleep in. They were far too poor for that.

Mr Bucket was the only person in the family with a job. He worked in a toothpaste factory, where he sat all day long at a bench and screwed the little caps on to the tops of the tubes of toothpaste after the tubes had been filled. But a toothpaste cap-screwer is never paid very much money, and poor Mr Bucket, however hard he worked, and however fast he screwed on the caps, was never able to make enough to buy one half of the things that so large a family needed. There wasn't even enough money to buy proper food for them all. The only meals they could afford were bread and margarine for breakfast, boiled potatoes and cabbage for lunch, and cabbage soup for supper. Sundays were a bit better. They all looked forward to Sundays because then, although they had exactly the same, everyone was allowed a second helping.

The Buckets, of course, didn't starve, but every one of them – the two old grandfathers, the two old grandmothers, Charlie's father, Charlie's mother, and especially little Charlie himself – went about from morning till night with a horrible empty feeling in their tummies.

Charlie felt it worst of all. And although his father and mother often went without their own share of lunch or supper so that they could give it to him, it still wasn't nearly enough for a growing boy. He desperately wanted something more filling and satisfying than cabbage and cabbage soup. The one thing he longed for more than anything else was . . . CHOCOLATE.

Walking to school in the mornings, Charlie could see great slabs of chocolate piled up high in the shop windows, and he would stop and stare and press his nose against the glass, his mouth watering like mad. Many times a day, he would see other children taking bars of creamy chocolate out of their pockets and munching them greedily, and *that*, of course, was *pure* torture.

Only once a year, on his birthday, did Charlie Bucket ever get to taste a bit of chocolate. The whole family saved up their money for that special occasion, and when the great day arrived, Charlie was always presented with one small chocolate bar to eat all by himself. And each time he received it, on those marvellous birthday mornings, he would place it carefully in a small wooden box that he owned, and treasure it as though it were a bar of solid gold; and for the next few days, he would allow himself only to look at it, but never to touch it. Then at last, when he could stand it no longer, he would peel back a *tiny* bit of the paper wrapping at one corner to expose a *tiny* bit of chocolate, and then he would take a *tiny* nibble – just enough to allow the lovely sweet taste to spread out slowly over his tongue. The next day, he would take another tiny nibble, and so on, and so on. And in this way, Charlie would make his sixpenny bar of birthday chocolate last him for more than a month.

But I haven't yet told you about the one awful thing that tortured little Charlie, the lover of chocolate, more than *anything* else. This thing, for him, was far, far worse than seeing slabs of chocolate in the shop windows or watching other children munching bars of creamy chocolate right in front of him. It was the most terrible torturing thing you could imagine, and it was this:

In the town itself, actually within *sight* of the house in which Charlie lived, there was an ENORMOUS CHOCOLATE FACTORY!

Just imagine that!

And it wasn't simply an ordinary enormous chocolate factory, either. It was the largest and most famous in the whole world! It was WONKA'S FACTORY, owned by a man called Mr Willy Wonka, the greatest inventor and maker of chocolates that there has ever been. And what a tremendous, marvellous place it was! It had huge iron gates leading into it, and a high wall surrounding it, and smoke belching from its chimneys, and strange whizzing sounds coming from deep inside it. And outside the walls, for half a mile around in every direction, the air was scented with the heavy rich smell of melting chocolate!

Twice a day, on his way to and from school, little Charlie Bucket had to walk right past the gates of the factory. And every time he went by, he would begin to walk very, very slowly, and he would hold his nose high in the air and take long deep sniffs of the gorgeous chocolatey smell all around him.

Oh, how he loved that smell!

And oh, how he wished he could go inside the factory and see what it was like!

THE
ROALD DAHL
FOUNDATION

Doing **wonkalicious** things

*Providing practical support for children with
brain, blood and literacy problems*

What is the Roald Dahl Foundation?

As well as being a great storyteller, Roald Dahl was also a
man who gave generously of his time and money to help
people in need, especially children. After he died in 1990,
his widow, Felicity, set up the Roald Dahl Foundation to
continue this generous tradition. Our support spreads far
and wide. Since we began, the Foundation has given over
£4 million across the UK.

The Foundation aims to help children and young people in
practical ways and in three areas that were particularly
important to Roald Dahl during his
lifetime: neurology, haematology, and
literacy. We make grants to
hospitals and charities, as well as to
individual childrens and their families.

Supporting the
Roald Dahl Foundation

Funded partly through the Foundation's original endowment, we also benefit from a range of fundraising, most notably the national sponsored reading event Readathon®. In addition, we are proud of the Friends of Roald Dahl Foundation who arrange a programme of local events, the many school children who fundraise on our behalf and our Payroll Giving supporters. Finally, we are able to benefit from an ambitious programme of new orchestral music for children based on Roald Dahl's stories and rhymes, specially commissioned on our behalf.

To find out more about the Roald Dahl Foundation or to make an online donation visit our website at www.roalddahlfoundation.org.

The Roald Dahl Foundation is a registered charity no. 1004230

THE ROALD DAHL MUSEUM AND STORY CENTRE

"Tremendous Things Are In Store for You!"

Are you one of Roald Dahl's biggest fans? If you are, then we have got some splendiferous news for you!

As you probably know, Roald Dahl lived in Great Missenden, a quiet village in Buckinghamshire where he wrote all of his stories for kids. But did you know that in spring 2005, Great Missenden will become the most scrumdiddlyumptious place in the world when the Roald Dahl Museum and Story Centre opens its doors for the first time!

The Museum and Story Centre will tell the eventful tale of Roald Dahl's life, using photographs and film. Interactive displays will help you to discover more about his Norwegian family, his schooldays, his time as a World War Two pilot and how he became a world-famous writer. It will also be jam-packed with stuff about how to write, a replica of Roald's writing hut and facts about other brilliant authors. There will even be a chance to make up stories of your own!

architect's impression of the Museum by Hawkins/Brown

At the heart of the Museum and Story Centre will be an amazing archive full of things that have never been seen before, including the original handwritten drafts of many of Roald's books, corrected typescripts, fifty years of letters, and a lifetime of family photographs.

For more information and to see how work on the Roald Dahl Museum and Story Centre is progressing, visit www.roalddahlmuseum.org.

Esio Trot

Mr Hoppy wished more than ever... that he could ... become a tortoise.

Have you ever wanted to turn into something else? I bet it wasn't a tortoise! This is the story of a very shy man who's in love with a very kind woman, and of the small tortoise who brings them together.

'*Esio Trot* reveals Roald Dahl at his sunniest and best . . . Quentin Blake's drawings make a perfect accompaniment' – *The Times*

George's Marvellous Medicine

You're growing too fast. Boys who grow too fast become stupid and lazy.'

Geeorge's grandma has some pretty odd views. In fact, she's not a very nice person at all. She thinks caterpillars and slugs are delicious and likes to crunch on beetles best of all. George can do nothing right in Grandma's eyes, so when it's time for her medicine he decides to give her a dose of his own special brew.

James
and the
Giant Peach

disgusting little beast

filthy nuisance

hideous brat

James's aunts, Spiker and Sponge, are always calling him names. They beat him and starve him and make his life a misery. If only his parents hadn't been eaten by an angry escaped rhinoceros, he wouldn't be in this mess. But one day he meets a mysterious man who gives him a bag of magic crocodile tongues and so begins the adventure of his dreams.

Fantastic Mr Fox

Boggis and Bunce and Bean

One fat, one short, one lean.

These horrible crooks

So different in looks

Were none the less equally mean.

Boggis, Bunce and Bean are the nastiest three farmers you could ever meet. They hate Mr Fox and plan to shoot, starve or dig him out of his hole. But Mr Fox is much cleverer than they are and he has a cunning plan of his own.

The Twits

Worms in spaghetti

Frogs in beds

Eyeballs in drinks

Mr and Mrs Twit play some horrible tricks on each other. I bet you have never met two people more revolting. They never wash, they trap birds for Bird Pie and they hate children. Find out what brilliant trick the Roly-Poly Bird and the Muggle-Wump monkeys think up for them.

The Giraffe and the Pelly and Me

What does a window-cleaning company need?

A bucket, a ladder and a cleaner?
How about a pelican, a giraffe and a monkey?
Not the usual ingredients, but this is a
window-cleaning company
with a difference. Join Billy
as he makes friends with three
amazing animals and gets
up to some thrilling
adventures.

Matilda

cheat
stupid
ignorant
liar

Matilda's parents have called her some terrible things. The truth is, she's a genius and they're the stupid ones. Find out how she gets the better of them and her spiteful headmistress, Miss Trunchbull, as well as discovering that she has a very special power.

Winner of the Children's Book Award

Read more in Puffin

For complete information about books available from Puffin – and Penguin – and how to order them, contact us at the appropriate address below. Please note that for copyright reasons the selection of books varies from country to country.

www.puffin.co.uk

In the United Kingdom: Please write to Dept EP, Penguin Books Ltd, Bath Road, Harmondsworth, West Drayton, Middlesex UB7 ODA

In the United States: Please write to Penguin Group (USA), Inc., P.O. Box 12289, Dept B, Newark, New Jersey 07101–5289 or call 1–800–788–6262

In Canada: Please write to Penguin Books Canada Ltd, 10 Alcorn Avenue, Suite 300, Toronto, Ontario M4V 3B2

In Australia: Please write to Penguin Books Australia Ltd, 250 Camberwell Road, Camberwell, Victoria 3124

In New Zealand: Please write to Penguin Books (NZ) Ltd, Private Bag 102902, North Shore Mail Centre, Auckland 10

In India: Please write to Penguin Books India Pvt Ltd, 11 Panscheel Shopping Centre, Panscheel Park, New Delhi 110 017

In the Netherlands: Please write to Penguin Books Netherlands bv, Postbus 3507, NL–1001 AH Amsterdam

In Germany: Please write to Penguin Books Deutschland GmbH, Metzlerstrasse 26, 60594 Frankfurt am Main

In Spain: Please write to Penguin Books S. A., Bravo Murillo 19, 1° B, 28015 Madrid

In Italy: Please write to Penguin Italia s.r.l., Via Felice Casati 20, I–20124 Milano

In France: Please write to Penguin France S. A., 17 rue Lejeune, F–31000 Toulouse

In Japan: Please write to Penguin Books Japan, Ishikiribashi Building, 2–5–4, Suido, Bunkyo-ku, Tokyo 112

In South Africa: Please write to Longman Penguin Southern Africa (Pty) Ltd, Private Bag X08, Bertsham 2013